AF269682

Solids, Liquids, and Gases

Kaitlyn Duling

rourkeeducationalmedia.com

BEFORE AND DURING READING ACTIVITIES

Before Reading: *Building Background Knowledge and Vocabulary*

Building background knowledge can help children process new information and build upon what they already know. Before reading a book, it is important to tap into what children already know about the topic. This will help them develop their vocabulary and increase their reading comprehension.

Questions and Activities to Build Background Knowledge:

1. Look at the front cover of the book and read the title. What do you think this book will be about?
2. What do you already know about this topic?
3. Take a book walk and skim the pages. Look at the table of contents, photographs, captions, and bold words. Did these text features give you any information or predictions about what you will read in this book?

Vocabulary: *Vocabulary Is Key to Reading Comprehension*

Use the following directions to prompt a conversation about each word.
- Read the vocabulary words.
- What comes to mind when you see each word?
- What do you think each word means?

Vocabulary Words:
- *describe*
- *helium*
- *matter*
- *observe*

During Reading: *Reading for Meaning and Understanding*

To achieve deep comprehension of a book, children are encouraged to use close reading strategies. During reading, it is important to have children stop and make connections. These connections result in deeper analysis and understanding of a book.

Close Reading a Text

During reading, have children stop and talk about the following:
- Any confusing parts
- Any unknown words
- Text to text, text to self, text to world connections
- The main idea in each chapter or heading

Encourage children to use context clues to determine the meaning of any unknown words. These strategies will help children learn to analyze the text more thoroughly as they read.

When you are finished reading this book, turn to the last page for an **After Reading Activity**.

Table of Contents

What Is Matter?

Let's find some **matter**.

It is everywhere.

There are three types of matter.

We can sort them. Solids are
one type.

A solid has a shape. Rocks, trees, and grass are solids.

Solids can be hard or soft.

Looking at Liquids

Water is a liquid. We can swim in liquids.

We can drink some liquids.

11

I pour juice into a cup.

What can we **observe** about
a liquid?

13

A liquid fills its container. How can we **describe** this liquid?

Milk is white and creamy.

15

Invisible Gases

The third type of matter is a gas. We can't see most gases.

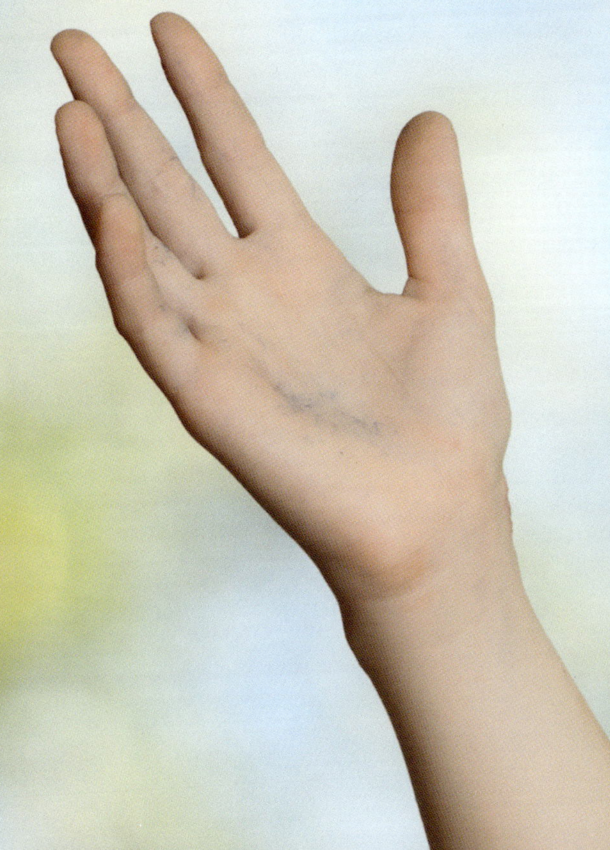

We might be able to smell them or breathe them in, like air.

Gases fill up space.

These balloons are full of **helium**.

What types of matter can you find?

Photo Glossary

describe (di-SKRIBE): Tell about something so that your listener gets an understanding of it.

helium (HEE-lee-uhm): A light, clear gas that does not burn. It is used to make balloons rise.

matter (MAT-ur): Anything that has weight and takes up space. It can be a solid, a liquid, or a gas.

observe (uhb-ZURV): To watch something closely in order to learn about it.

Dessert Matters

Make a sweet treat that includes a solid, a liquid, and a gas!

Supplies

root beer
tall glass
vanilla ice cream

Directions

1. With an adult's help, pour a glass about half full of root beer. This is a liquid.
2. Carefully add a small scoop of ice cream. Before it melts, the ice cream is a solid.
3. Now look closely at the cup. Do you see the bubbles? The bubbles are the gas in your dessert. This gas is called carbon dioxide.

Index

About the Author

Kaitlyn Duling is an avid reader and writer who grew up in Illinois. She now resides in Washington, D.C. Kaitlyn has written over 60 books for children and teens. You can learn more about her at www.kaitlynduling.com.

After Reading Activity

Look around the room. How many different types of matter do you see? Do you see any liquids? Are there gases in the room, including air? Draw a picture of the room, labeling the different types of matter.

Library of Congress PCN Data

Solids, Liquids, and Gases / Kaitlyn Duling
(My Physical Science Library)
ISBN 978-1-73161-412-4 (hard cover)(alk. paper)
ISBN 978-1-73161-207-6 (soft cover)
ISBN 978-1-73161-517-6 (e-Book)
ISBN 978-1-73161-622-7 (e-Pub)
Library of Congress Control Number: 2019932068

Rourke Educational Media
Printed in the United States of America,
North Mankato, Minnesota

www.rourkeeducationalmedia.com

Edited by: Kim Thompson
Produced by Blue Door Education for Rourke Educational Media.
Cover and interior design by: Nicola Stratford

Photo Credits: Cover logo: frog © Eric Phol, test tube © Sergey Lazarev, cover tab art © siridhata, cover photo: © JPC-PROD, cover balloon G © Cute little things, page background art © Zaie; pages Page 5 © 2xSamara.com; page 6 © japansainlook, page 7 © morisfoto; page 8 © Wisanu_nuu, page 9 © Plateon; page 10 © YanLev, page 11 © vystekimages; page 13 © Roxana Bashyrova; page 15 © Pavlo Lys; page 16-17 © p_ponomareva; page 19 © Africa Studio; page 21 © Rawpixel.com; page 22 top left © Monkey Business Images, bottom right© ESB Professional All images from Shutterstock.com